THE DRAGON'S BREAKFAST

VIVIAN FRENCH

illustrated by Marta Kissi

WALKER
BOOKS

This is a work of fiction. Names, characters, places and incidents are either the product of the author's imagination or, if real, are used fictitiously. All statements, activities, stunts, descriptions, information and material of any other kind contained herein are included for entertainment purposes only and should not be relied on for accuracy or replicated as they may result in injury.

First published 2019 by Walker Books Ltd
87 Vauxhall Walk, London SE11 5HJ

2 4 6 8 10 9 7 5 3 1

This book has been typeset in Berkeley Oldstyle Book

Printed and bound by CPI Group (UK) Ltd, Croydon CR0 4YY

British Library Cataloguing in Publication Data:
a catalogue record for this book is available from the British Library

ISBN 978-1-4063-7936-5

www.walker.co.uk

For Princess Freya Elisavet Bluebell Bythell

May you find magic and tame dragons

wherever you go.

For my beloved husband, James

M.K.

Chapter One

"Yeuch! My egg's runny!" Prince Dribble threw down his spoon. "It's horrible and I won't eat it! Not ever!" He pulled at the tablecloth and only a well-timed grab by the queen saved the breakfast plates, cups and bowls from crashing to the floor.

"I want toast! And I want it NOW!" The heir to the kingdom of Strüggen stuck out his lower lip and scowled.

"There, there, my poppet," his mother soothed. "Of course you can have toast. Lots and lots of toast. As much as you can eat. Now, would my precious one like raspberry jam or strawberry?"

Dribble considered the question. "Want honey."

Queen Hyacinth snapped her fingers at the nearest serving boy. "You! Fetch a pot of honey right now this minute! And a large plate of buttered toast, lightly browned, with the crusts cut off!" The boy hesitated and the queen frowned. "I haven't seen you before, have I? What's your name?"

"No, ma'am. I'm Billy, ma'am. I'm new here. Um … which way's the kitchen?"

The queen pointed at a door and Billy disappeared at speed, only to reappear a few minutes later looking agonized.

"If you please, ma'am, Cook says there isn't any

honey. There's only strawberry jam."

"I don't want strawberry!" Dribble turned purple, picked up his cup and hurled it at Billy. "Go and find a bee and MAKE me some honey!"

Billy, failing to see the queen's warning glance as he hopped out of the way of the flying cup, shook his head. "If you please, and 'scuse me for mentioning it, but honey doesn't quite come that easy…"

The prince gave an ear-piercing scream and flung himself onto the carpet, kicking his short fat legs. "I want honey! I want honey!"

His mother glared at Billy. "Just look what you've done! You've upset the prince! What's your name again?"

The boy was very pale. "Billy, ma'am. From the orphanage. Mr Sackage sent me."

"Well, Billy, you're a failure. I don't want you here in the palace. You're dismissed."

Queen Hyacinth gave an imperious wave that sent Billy running for the door. Once there, he stopped.

"I'm very sorry, ma'am. I really am. I don't suppose there's any chance you might change your mind? Only, I don't know what I'll do. Mr Sackage won't let me back in the orphanage and I've nowhere to go…"

"Absolutely not." The queen rose up from her seat. "I never change my mind, not ever – and if you don't go away right now this minute, I'll throw you in the dungeon!"

Prince Dribble stopped wailing and sat up looking hopeful. "Put him in the dungeon, Ma! Put him in the deep dark dungeon with the big scary spiders."

"That's so not fair!"

Billy jumped and the queen looked astonished. The voice had come from under the table – it belonged to a girl. She was wearing a faded frilly dress that was much too small for her, and her hair was wispy and needed brushing.

"Princess Persephone! What ARE you doing under the table?" Queen Hyacinth's voice was cold.

The princess wriggled out from under the table and stood up. "I always have my breakfast under there," she said. "Who'd want to risk being covered in egg by a horrid little brat? Not me. And it's not the boy's fault there isn't any honey, Mother. The brat ate it all with a teaspoon when Cook wasn't looking. So you shouldn't send the boy away!"

Prince Dribble, who had been listening with his mouth hanging open, suddenly realized his sister was talking about him. He turned an ugly crimson and began to scream so loudly there was no chance of hearing Queen Hyacinth's reply … but her expression was far from encouraging.

Billy didn't wait. He fled – and the princess ran after him.

Chapter Two

As Billy headed down the long marble corridor that led to the back door of the palace, the princess caught up with him. "Boy! Do stop! I want to talk to you!"

Billy slowed a little. "What for?"

"I want to know what you're going to do! You said you had nowhere to go."

"I haven't." Billy stopped and looked at the girl. She didn't look like a princess. With her faded dress and wild hair, she looked much more like one of the girls from the orphanage. "Are you really a princess?"

"Yes. It's awful. I'm Princess Persephone Stephanie Tiffany Jane … and I wish I wasn't. Mother hates me because I'm not a boy and I don't think Father even remembers I exist. He's much too busy worrying about his stupid warships." Persephone tucked her arm into Billy's and they began to walk together. "You can call me 'Pom'. What's your name?"

"Billy. Billy Boiler." Billy waited for the princess to laugh, but she didn't.

"So, Billy Boiler – what are you going to do now?"

Billy shrugged. He was aware of an uncomfortable sinking feeling when he thought about his future. "I don't know."

"I don't know what I'm going to do either," Pom told him. "I hate it here. I've been wondering about running away to the orphanage. Do you think they'd take me in?"

"The orphanage?" Billy's eyes widened. "But you're not an orphan! You've got a mother and a father."

Pom made a face. "I'd lie, stupid. I'm good at that. I'd tell them ever such a sad story about my father being lost at sea and my mother being eaten by a shark when she swam out to look for him. It would make them terribly sorry for me."

"No, it wouldn't." Billy shook his head. "Mr Sackage never feels sorry for anyone. Not ever. And he'd most likely send you straight here to be a nursery maid, because that's what he does with all the girls. He only sent me because there weren't any girls left and he wanted his five pound fee."

"Oh." Pom frowned. "That wouldn't be much fun. Mother would be absolutely furious and I'd be back with the revolting brat. I couldn't bear that. I think I'd better run away with you, instead. Would you mind?"

Billy's head was reeling. He'd been hauled out of bed early that morning with the news that he was leaving the orphanage for ever and going to work in the palace … and now not only had he lost his job, but a princess he had known for just ten minutes was suggesting that they ran away together.

"Ummm," he said.

Pom withdrew her arm. "I'll think of something else, then." She sounded hurt and Billy was immediately remorseful.

"I'm sorry. It's just … it's just that I didn't think a princess would bother with someone like me. I've never met a princess before, you see."

"Well, now you have." Pom gave him a thoughtful look. "I do hope you're not going to be silly about all that royalty stuff. It doesn't mean anything, you know. Wearing a crown and living in a palace doesn't make you a nice person." She sighed. "If anything, I'd say it does the opposite. I mean, think about that disgusting brother of mine. What he needs is a good hard slap … or at least someone to say no to him sometimes. But Mother lets him do exactly what he wants."

Billy nodded, but didn't like to agree too enthusiastically in case it was wrong to be rude about a prince.

Pom raised her eyebrows. "You do think he's revolting, don't you? It's okay to say so. I won't put you in the dungeon with the big scary spiders."

"I didn't like him much," Billy admitted – and Pom snorted.

"He's vile. So … I think we'd better run away, don't you? Where shall we go?"

This was hard for Billy to answer. His world had

never extended far beyond the cold stone walls of the orphanage and he'd never had a geography lesson in his life. As he searched his mind for an idea, Mr Sackage swam into his thoughts. Mr Sackage shouting, Mr Sackage swearing … and Mr Sackage threatening that if Billy didn't behave himself, he'd be sent to— where was it?

"Bullion Island," Billy said.

"What?" Pom stared at him as if he'd said they should go to the moon. "Do you really mean that?"

Billy nodded, hoping he looked as if he knew what he was talking about. "Yes."

"Bullion Island." Pom's eyes began to shine. "Why not? Hey, Billy – you're not nearly as silly as you look, are you? I'd never have thought of that. Not in a million years! Nobody ever, ever, EVER goes to Bullion!" And seizing Billy's arm, she began to run.

"Hang on a minute!" Billy's feet were dragging. "What do you mean, nobody ever goes there? What's wrong with it?"

Pom stopped so suddenly that Billy almost ran into her. "You mean – you don't know?" She sounded so incredulous that Billy blinked.

"No." Billy swallowed. "Is it … *dangerous*?"

"Dangerous?" Pom nodded enthusiastically. "Yes, ever so dangerous!"

Billy's stomach turned a somersault. "But why? Tell me about Bullion Island."

"It's why we hate Thrum," Pom said. "And why Father keeps building ships. One day soon there's going to be a terrible war between Strüggen and Thrum. They think Bullion belongs to them, but it doesn't. It definitely belongs to Strüggen … at least, that's what Father says."

Billy was puzzled. "But why do you want it so much?"

Pom leant towards him. "Gold! There's a simply enormous stash of gold! Ages and ages ago, Pirate Jed Josiah Jones hid his boxes of treasure on Bullion Island. There's enough to make every single person in Strüggen rich, rich, RICH!"

"But if there's such a lot of treasure," Billy said, "why can't you share it with Thrum?"

"Share it?" Pom looked at him in astonishment. "Kingdoms NEVER share!" She gave her companion a patronizing smile. "You don't know much, do you, Billy?"

"I don't suppose I do," Billy agreed meekly. Another thought came to him. "So why doesn't someone sail over in the dark when they can't be seen?"

"People have tried." Pom shook her head. "A long, long time ago they tried, but—" she lowered her voice. "Only empty ships came back. And guess what? Smoke floated up from the island!"

"Smoke?" Billy's voice was a whisper.

"*Smoke*," Pom repeated. "So there's something

guarding the gold and Father says he's almost sure that it's—" she paused for effect— "a dragon!"

"A dragon?" Billy's eyes were as round as saucers. "Has anyone seen it?"

Pom sighed. "No. It's very disappointing. But smoke puffs up every so often. And THAT, Billy Boiler, is why Bullion is very, very dangerous… And why we're going to go and find out what's there!"

And before Billy could ask any more questions, she opened the palace door and pushed him outside.

Chapter Three

Queen Planchette of Thrum was striding round the battlements of the royal castle. This was something she enjoyed enormously, as she could see her small kingdom laid out beneath her: the Cowering Hills in the north marked the border, then came the neatly laid out farms and fields where most of her subjects lived, and finally there was the line of jagged rocks that edged the harbour, where a dozen small warships bobbed and bowed on the incoming tide.

As Queen Planchette's gaze fell on them, she smiled proudly. "My fine defenders! And every one of them ready to set sail!" She squinted across the sea to where a low-lying landmass broke the horizon, and shook her fist. "Strüggen! I defy you!"

"Hurrah! You tell them!"

The queen swung round, frowning. "Jangle! I do wish you wouldn't creep up on me like that. Where are your bells? You're meant to be a jester, aren't you? Jesters wear bells."

Jangle, an exceptionally large boy dressed in jesters' red and yellow, shrugged. "The goat ate them."

"The goat?" The queen's eyebrows rose. "What goat?"

"The goat you made prime minister." Jangle looked smug. "I told you it wasn't a good idea."

Planchette stared for a moment, then began to laugh until she was shaking all over.

Jangle had been sent to the castle by his parents, in the hope that he might learn a useful trade; the queen had been doubtful about his potential at first, but a large donation from his father had persuaded her that she needed a jester. Jangle himself was not at all enthusiastic about this arrangement: Planchette expected him to work in exchange for his board and lodging, and work was not something he approved of.

The queen, in his opinion, didn't eat enough cake. Or meringues. Or chocolate biscuits. Or any of the other delicious things that Jangle had expected to find on a royal tea table as compensation for having to wear a red and yellow suit with bells on.

"But Jangle," Planchette said at last, "think how much better a goat is than that ancient niminy-pinnie I had before! The goat doesn't answer back, he doesn't make silly suggestions and he never ever asks me for money!"

Jangle scowled. "But he eats everything. It's not just my jesters' bells – he ate my breakfast! AND he's eaten all the cushions on your throne. AND the curtains, as far as he could reach. AND he chomped up the papers on your desk."

"Really?" Planchette stopped smiling. "That's extremely thoughtless of him. Perhaps you'd better take him back to his field … although that means I'll have to find someone else to be prime minister."

"Put up a notice," Jangle suggested.

"I suppose so." The queen sounded doubtful, but a sudden thought came to her and she clapped her hands. "Jangle! YOU can be prime minister. I can't imagine why I didn't think of it before – perhaps it was the bells that distracted me. YOU can be prime minister and we'll let the goat be the court-jester … in his field, of course. I can't afford new cushions and curtains now, let alone on a regular basis."

"Me?" Jangle was horrified. "But I can't! Pa sent me here to learn to be a jester and I don't know anything about prime-ministering. Besides, I'm not old enough!"

"Rubbish, Jangle. You're older than the goat, aren't you? Now, stop arguing and come down to the harbour with me. It's time to inspect the ships!"

Jangle didn't answer; he was looking out to sea. "What's that smoke?"

The queen turned round. "Smoke? Where? You don't mean Strüggen, do you? Oh … oh dear. It's Bullion Island."

Jangle looked at her in surprise. "What's the matter?"

"Don't you know?" Planchette's gaze was fixed on the greenish smoke, floating up into the sky. "Whatever do they teach you in school these days? It's a warning … a warning not to land on Bullion. It's a warning to leave the gold alone."

Jangle snorted in disbelief. "Gold? That's a fairy story, that is."

"It's true," the queen said. "There really is gold there – lots and lots of it. It's Pirate Jed Josiah Jones's treasure and there's enough to make every man, woman and child in Thrum rich beyond their wildest dreams. But we never send our ships out, because we're terrified of disturbing whatever it is that lives on the island. I'm sure it's a dragon… Dragons are attracted by gold, you see – and dragons breathe smoke."

Jangle shrugged. "It can't be a dragon. My mum says there aren't any left."

Planchette raised an eyebrow. "Is that so? Well, let's hope she's right. But my father thought there was a dragon and he told me that, chances are, one day it'll get bored with puffing out smoke and fly away … and THAT'S when we'll go to war with Strüggen. They think the gold belongs to them, but it doesn't – it belongs to Thrum." She paused and a thoughtful look came over her face.

"Jangle, I've had an idea. I think we should send someone to Bullion Island to see what's going on. My spies can't see what's happening on the south side, and who knows? Maybe a boat has sneaked across from Strüggen and *that's* why there's smoke. I can't send one of my warships – that would be sure to cause trouble if it turns out to be a false alarm. The king of Strüggen has spies all along the coastline. But a canoe, or a small rowing boat, might not be noticed if it went at night. What do you think?"

Jangle hadn't been listening. His stomach was rumbling, and he had been wondering if he could have a fortifying snack before they went to inspect the fleet. "Oh, yes," he said cheerfully. "Brilliant idea. You're quite right."

"Excellent." The queen nodded. "It's always reassuring when one's prime minister agrees with one. You can go tonight. When we get to the harbour, we'll look for an insignificant little boat."

Jangle's jaw dropped. "ME?"

"Of course. You're my prime minister, aren't you? And you said yourself, it's a brilliant idea. So there we are: all settled. Now, let's go and inspect the fleet."

Queen Planchette strode away, with a highly agitated Jangle trailing behind her.

Chapter Four

Billy and Pom were standing on the harbour wall, arguing about the best way to get to Bullion Island, when Pom gave a sudden gasp.

"Look! SMOKE! Can you see, Billy? Do you think it's the dragon? Oh … wouldn't that be absolutely wonderful?"

Billy swallowed. He was wondering if he'd made a terrible mistake; Pom didn't seem to be afraid of anything, whereas he could see problems round every corner. She had wanted to help herself to one of the small fishing boats tied up at the harbour side – Billy had protested that this was stealing, and Pom had called him a "ninny-hammer" and told him that adventurers always took risks.

"*Besides,*" she had added, "*we'll bring it back. Sometime or other.*"

I expect it's because she's a princess, Billy told himself. *She doesn't know what it's like to have things stolen.* Out loud he said, "We could ask that man over there, maybe."

The man Billy was looking at was cleaning out a small rowing boat, muttering as he did so. Pom pranced up to him, doing her best to smile persuasively. "I'm Princess Persephone," she began, "and I really need to borrow a boat—"

The man looked up, scowling. "One of them royals, are you? Don't hold with them, I don't. Never does nothing for us."

Pom clapped her hands, making the man jump. "Oh, you're absolutely right! I hate them too. Me and Billy – Billy's that boy standing with his mouth hanging open – me and Billy are running away to Bullion Island to get away from them!"

"Bullion?" The man blinked. "There's a big fearsome dragon there, or so the old folks say."

"That's why we're going!" This time Pom's smile was genuine. "We want to see if he's real!"

"You do, do you?" The man stood up. "But what if you gets eaten? Likely as not I'll get the blame."

Pom shook her head. "Just say we took your boat when you weren't looking. They're sure to believe you. I'm always taking things without asking."

Much to Billy's surprise, the man gave a loud guffaw of laughter before picking up the oars and handing them to Pom. "Here you go. I likes plain talking. If you find a whole heap of treasure, you make sure you bring a bit back for me. Digger Lamputt's the name. Don't you go forgetting, now!"

"We won't!" Pom was ecstatic. "And thank you! Thank you so much!" She turned to Billy. "Come on! Hop in!"

Billy did as he was told. "Is it safe? It's very wobbly!" He sat down with a bump and looked anxiously at Pom as she took hold of the oars.

"I'll give you a push out," Digger said and he gave the little boat such a shove that Billy shut his eyes, expecting to be drowned at any moment. There was no surge of sea water, however, and when he opened his eyes again he found they were safely bobbing over the waves.

Pom was surprisingly good at rowing; a couple of times she splashed Billy, but they made steady progress towards the island. Billy, watching the shore grow gradually nearer and nearer, was trying his hardest not to feel sick.

What if the dragon rushed at them? He wasn't brave, like Pom. He knew he'd run away. And could dragons swim? Were they safe in the boat? It was such a very small boat…

He took a deep breath. *This is an adventure*, he told himself. *After all, if I wasn't here, I'd be back in the orphanage. Or … or I don't know where.* He took another breath. *I'm on an adventure, so I must try to be adventurous…*

"Billy – are you okay?" Pom had stopped rowing in order to inspect him. "You've gone a funny colour. Are you feeling seasick?"

"No!" Billy said, rather louder than he'd meant to. "I'm fine!"

Pom began to row again. "Good," she said, "because we're nearly there … and we're going to have to be careful." She grinned cheerfully. "It's wonderfully scary, isn't it? I'm terrified! Can you see somewhere we can land?"

"It looks very rocky." Billy tried not to sound anxious. "Big rocks, too, and ever so sharp…"

"Billy!" Pom shook her head at him. "Stop worrying! Just look for a way in."

Billy nodded. A moment later he sat up straight and pointed. "Over there! There's a little beach."

Pom swung the boat round so she could see. "Perfect," she said. "Here we go! Five more minutes and we'll be on Bullion Island … OH!"

"What is it?" Billy asked.

Pom was crossing her eyes and scowling. "It's nothing." She turned the boat and began rowing again. "I just noticed there's a cave at the top of the beach. It might be useful if we need somewhere to hide."

Billy, hoping very much that they wouldn't ever have a reason to hide, made a non-committal noise as the boat drew nearer and nearer to the small shingle beach.

There was a scrunching noise and Pom slipped over the side into the water. "Come on, help me pull the boat up the shore."

"But I can't swim," Billy said.

Pom laughed. "It's only ankle-deep, silly. Look, I'm standing up."

"Oh … okay." Billy lowered himself into the clear blue shallows, and together he and Pom hauled the rowing boat out of the water.

"There!" Pom tucked the oars neatly inside. "And now, let's explore – and hope we can find the dragon." And without waiting to see if Billy was following, she began to scramble up the rocks.

Billy was about to climb after her when a movement caught his eye. He looked round – and froze. Something was creeping out of the cave … something covered in long matted greenish-grey fur, with claw-like hands and feet.

Billy's heart began to pound; much too frightened to move, he shut his eyes tightly in the hope that the monster might quietly go away.

"Urrrrr," growled a voice. "You on them rocks. Is you helping me?"

Billy didn't answer: he was certain he was about to be eaten alive. His mouth was so dry that he couldn't call to Pom for help. All he could do was wait for a scaly hand to clutch at his legs.

There was a long silence.

Billy began to breathe again, but dared not move.

The silence continued … and then there was a sob.

Billy was so surprised he opened his eyes – and saw the monster was sitting at the mouth of the cave, its furry face wet with tears. As he looked, it began to rock itself from side to side, wailing.

"**Nobody does love us! Nobody does! We is ugly, ugly, ugly, and nobody does ever speak to us ... nobody loves poor Mumble. They makes faces when they sees us, they does. They crosses their eyes! Nobody help. Nobody, nobody, nobody.**"

Billy knew all too well what it felt like to be unhappy, and to have nobody care about you. He moved cautiously towards the cave. "Don't cry. Oh, please don't cry! What's the matter? Why do you need help?"

The monster peered through its long greenish fur at Billy, then slowly held out one of its scaly paws. A piece of fishing line was wound round so tightly that it had cut into the scales, and the paw was red and swollen.

Billy winced. "Ouch! That looks ever so sore. Here … hold still and I'll see if I can undo it."

"**Urrrrr**." The monster did as it was told and Billy began to battle with the knots. The line was tough and deeply embedded, but gradually Billy managed to untangle it. His fingers were sore and his arms were aching by the time the final knot was untied.

"There," he said and sat back on his heels. "You're free. Erm … what's your name?"

"**Urrrrrr. We is a Mumble.**" The monster shook its paw, then began licking it. "**Who you?**"

"I'm Billy," Billy told him. "Billy Boiler. How do you do?"

The Mumble sighed heavily. "**We does badly. We is Mumble, we is ugly. They laughs at us, they do, and they makes faces.**"

"Who makes faces at you?" Billy glanced nervously behind him.

Before the Mumble could answer, there was a slithering noise and Pom slid down the rocks. "BILLY! What are you DOING? I've been waiting and waiting for you!"

"I was talking to a Mumble," Billy said. "Look—oh! He's gone!"

Billy was right. There was no sign of the creature.

"You were talking to a what?" Pom frowned. "Billy – are you telling fibs?"

"No!" Billy was indignant. "I don't tell fibs!"

As Pom still looked doubtful, Billy bent down at the cave entrance. "Mumble!" he called. "Mumble? It's okay … this is a friend of mine! She won't hurt you!"

"**Urrrrr...**" The growl from the darkness made Pom jump. "**Urrrrrr … her did make faces at us. Her did see us when you was in little boatie-boat!**"

Billy turned to Pom, who was looking hard at the ground. "You saw the Mumble? But you never said anything. You never warned me!"

Pom's cheeks were very pink as she shrugged. "It ran away when I made a face at it, so it obviously wasn't all that scary. I didn't tell you because I didn't want to risk you making a fuss." Her cheeks grew even pinker. "I thought you might not want to land on Bullion, you see – that you'd want to go home. And I do SO want to have an adventure. But you've made friends with it now, so it's fine!"

Billy opened his mouth to say it *wasn't* fine, then decided not to. Perhaps this was how princesses behaved? And besides, she was right.

He allowed himself a small glow of pride. He, Billy Boiler, had met a monster and he hadn't run away. What's more he had been able to help him.

"**What you doing now?**" The Mumble was at the entrance of the cave.

"We're going to find the dragon!" Pom announced. "There is one, isn't there?"

The Mumble paused, then said, "**There be dragon.**"

"YES!" Pom punched the air. "Did you hear that, Billy? There really is a dragon! Hey, Mumble – is it enormous? Does it breathe fire? Is it very fierce?"

Billy had noticed the Mumble's hesitation in answering. "What's wrong?" he asked. "Something's wrong, isn't it?"

"**Is she,**" the Mumble said. "**Dragon be she. She be big, she breathe fire too.**" It edged a little way out of its hiding place and beckoned to Billy to come closer. Billy did as he was told, but when Pom followed him the Mumble growled loudly. "**Urrrrr! Not she!**"

As Pom stepped back, Billy knelt down beside the Mumble. "What is it?"

"**You help us,**" the Mumble said. "**So us help you. No go find dragon. Her won't like it! Get in boatie-boat and go away. Get go now!**" And then, with a flurry of grit and small stones, the Mumble vanished into the darkness of the cave.

Billy looked at Pom, and Pom looked at Billy. "I heard what he told you," she said. "So what do you want to do? Run away? Or stay?" She pointed to the boat. "I'll take you back if you want to go. I know you're scared. I was mean not to tell you I saw the Mumble, and I'm sorry."

"No." Billy's mind was in such confusion he hardly knew what he was saying. Nobody had ever apologized to him before and he had never had a real friend; especially not a friend who asked him to share an adventure. But he was still suffering from a terrible feeling of dread. He had to swallow hard before he could manage a smile. "I want to stay."

Pom beamed at him. "Fantastic! Right … let's get up that cliff, and see what's there!"

They were puffing by the time they reached the top. It was a steep climb; as they crawled over the edge, they rolled into the rough grass, exhausted.

"Here we are!" Pom was jubilant. "And now to find the dragon!"

Billy sat up, hugging his knees. "Can I ask you something?"

Pom snorted. "Don't be silly. Of course you can!"

"Well … what are we going to do if we *do* find the dragon?" Billy hoped he didn't sound as nervous as he felt. "I mean, you don't want to take her home or anything?"

As soon as he had spoken he wished he hadn't. Pom leapt to her feet. "Billy Boiler, I'm so VERY

glad I met you! You have the best ideas ever. Just imagine Father's face if I bring a dragon back to Strüggen! He'd absolutely have to notice me then, wouldn't he? I'd be much more important than that horrid little brat… Oh, Billy – do let's!"

Billy's thoughts were whirling. Everything was telling him to say NO, it was a very BAD idea – but there was such a hopeful look on Pom's face that he found he couldn't. "Erm…" he said. "Perhaps we should see how big she is first?"

"Of course." Pom seemed happy with this suggestion, and Billy sighed with relief as she went on, "I've just realized I'm starving. Even my legs feel empty and I'll never be able to catch a dragon if I'm dying of hunger. What can we eat? There must be some berries, or mushrooms, or something. Didn't they teach you about things like that at the orphanage? How to find your own food?"

"No." Billy shook his head. "They didn't teach us much at all. And we mostly ate sloppy porridge."

Pom rolled her eyes. "Yuck. Oh well, we'll just have to experiment. We'll take it in turns to try things. I'll go first."

It took the two adventurers longer than they had hoped to find anything that looked even remotely edible, and the sun was sinking low in the west before they sat down in front of a collection of assorted berries, mushrooms and a few shriveled crab apples.

Pom selected a bright red berry, but quickly spat it out. "Yuck! Try one of the apples, Billy."

The apples were sour but bearably so, and were quickly eaten.

"My turn again," Pom announced. "I'll try a mushroom."

Billy had been studying the mushrooms and he put out a restraining hand. "I know I don't know anything – but aren't they meant to be brown? That one's blue."

"Only one way to find out," Pom said cheerfully and she nibbled at the edge of the large blue mushroom. "Hmmm … it's not bad. Kind of like … like … *mmmmmm…*"

Then, her eyes slowly closing, she slid down into the grass and began to snore.

"Pom? POM! Wake up! Oh, do please wake up!" Billy bent over his companion, but there was no response.

He tried shaking her, but that had no effect. He tried again and for a moment Pom's eyelids flickered … but then she settled herself into a more comfortable position and the snoring continued.

Billy picked up the mushroom and looked at it. Then he sniffed it. It smelled very much like an ordinary mushroom so, very cautiously, he licked it.

At once he felt dizzy, and he sat down with a thump.

The mushroom … I knew *there was something wrong with it!* He thought to himself, rubbing his eyes. *It's making my head feel as if it's stuffed full of cotton wool. And I'm sleepy – so sleepy.*

He yawned, then yawned again.

I'll just lie down while I wait for Pom to wake up. That would be sensible. Very … very … sensible…

And Billy curled up in the long grass like an exhausted puppy.

Chapter Five

Jangle tried all afternoon to persuade Queen Planchette that he was the most unsuitable adventurer ever, but with no success.

"For heaven's sake, Jangle! It's not as if I was expecting you to bring the dragon home in a paper bag! I just want you to row round the island and check that none of Strüggen's ships have sneaked across the Dillyman Sea. You don't have to put a foot on land."

Jangle gulped. "But what if there IS a ship? They might catch me!"

"I doubt they'd want you," Planchette said.

"But I really don't think you need worry. As soon as you get a clear view of the other side and see what's happening – if anything is, of course – you can come straight back and report to me."

Jangle went on arguing, but nothing he said could change the queen's mind.

When he said he couldn't row the queen promised him a sailing boat. When he said he didn't know how to work a sail boat, she said she'd ask the Royal Turtle to tow him. When Jangle said he was allergic to turtles and they gave him spots, she said she'd make sure the tow rope was very long.

"Now I come to think of it," said Planchette, "a turtle tow is by far the most sensible idea. A sail might be seen, and oars splash and make a noise. Alberta, on the other hand, is wonderfully silent when she swims." She winked at Jangle. "Just make sure you don't go singing any merry maritime songs! She'll sing along and she's got a voice like a foghorn."

Defeated, Jangle gave in. He spent the rest of the day sitting on the harbour-side, gloomily staring at the distant Bullion Island while eating bread and jam.

As the evening drew in, Jangle took himself off to the castle kitchen to collect a selection of cakes, buns and biscuits, to sustain him on his perilous voyage. The queen found him packing a basket and snatched it away from him.

"No, Jangle! Alberta's a very reliable turtle, but she's greedy. If you want a peaceful journey you'll leave those goodies behind. Now, come with me. Your boat's waiting and Alberta's being harnessed. If you go now, you should be back in plenty of time for hot chocolate before you go to bed."

Jangle reluctantly followed as Planchette strode away. He said nothing about the currant buns he had stuffed into his pockets.

I'm not going to starve, and that's that, he told himself. *A stupid turtle won't notice. It's a lot of fuss about nothing.*

Arriving at the harbour, he was alarmed to see how very small the boat was – and how very large the turtle.

"There!" The queen beamed at him. "The weather couldn't be better; the sea's as calm as a mill pond. You don't need to worry about a thing: Alberta will look after you, she's an exceptionally intelligent turtle. She'll tow you all the way … just remember to stay awake and watch out for anything suspicious."

She fished in her pocket and brought out a solid gold chain.

"I forgot to give you this before. Prime Minister Jangle, I wish you well on your mission."

And she hung the chain round Jangle's neck. Jangle didn't thank her – the chain weighed heavily, and his first thought was that if the boat sank he'd sink even faster.

Queen Planchette was unconcerned. She watched him clamber into the boat, and glanced up at the night sky.

"There's the moon coming up. Time to go!"

She blew sharply on a silver whistle and the turtle began to swim. Jangle had been expecting a sudden jerk as the rope grew taut, but the boat slipped away so smoothly he hardly noticed he was moving.

Gradually he felt confident enough to let go of the sides and sit up. Alberta was a dim shape ahead, surging steadily through the silver-tipped waves of the Dillyman Sea, and he began to feel pleased with himself. Here he was, Prime Minister of Thrum, going on an important mission on behalf of the queen.

The moon was high and very bright, and it occurred to him that he was meant to be keeping a look-out. Bullion was getting closer by the minute; Alberta had already changed course so they could circle the island. Jangle was delighted to see she was keeping well away from the shore, so it seemed unlikely that anything ferocious could reach him.

The island was peacefully shrouded in

night. He could see trees and rocks, and small, pleasingly empty beaches… There was no sign of enemy activity of any sort.

As Alberta swam steadily on and the south side of the island came into clear view, Jangle heaved a sigh of relief. The southern shoreline was as empty and uninhabited as the north.

There! I knew it was all a fuss about nothing, he told himself. *Not so much as a sandcastle. I bet there isn't even a dragon!* He yawned and rubbed his stomach. *I'm looking forward to my hot chocolate … oh! I almost forgot my snack. Just what I need to keep me going.*

He pulled a currant bun from his pocket and began to eat it with enthusiasm.

"Yummy!" he said. "Really yummy— Wait a minute. What's going on? That turtle's swimming the wrong way."

Alberta, her little black eyes gleaming, was heading towards him as fast as she could paddle. Jangle, alarmed, stood up.

"Get away!" he shouted. "Get back!"

Alberta took no notice. Currant buns were her favourite and she kept coming, her mouth open wide in anticipation. Jangle, convinced she was going to attack him, gave a terrified scream, leapt for safety ... and hit the water with an enormous

SPLASH!

The sea was cold – very cold. Jangle coughed and spluttered, and splashed madly in an attempt to frighten Alberta. Alberta, however, refused to

be scared. She had caught the remains of the bun and swallowed it in one gulp, and was now in a quandary as to what to do next. But leaving the Prime Minister of Thrum doggy-paddling in the Dillyman Sea was sure to upset Queen Planchette, so she made up her mind to rescue him.

Jangle was just as determined to get away from her, and as Alberta came closer he developed a surprising turn of speed; his plump arms whirled while his plump legs kicked up fountains of spray. Undeterred, Alberta dived down and came up underneath him, and the terrified Prime Minister of Thrum found himself balanced on the back of her shell.

"NO," he shrieked and, hurling himself back into the water, he struck out for land as fast as he could swim. In a matter of moments he felt shingle under his feet and he half-swam, half-paddled his way onto a beach. Once there he flung himself up the nearest rocks, whimpering as he climbed, and he didn't stop until he was quite certain he was out of harm's way.

Alberta, confused and hurt by this unfriendly behaviour, swam in a circle while she considered what she should do. She could see Jangle shivering on the top of the rocks; deciding that he wasn't going anywhere in a hurry, she waddled onto the shore and settled down to wait for him.

Jangle looked down and groaned. "It wants to eat me, I know it does! Can it climb?"

Deciding to play it safe, he scrambled to the top of the cliff. Once there he peered down again – Alberta was nibbling seaweed, and he shivered.

"Maybe it'll go to sleep and I can creep past to the boat? But what if it doesn't?" A sudden wild thought struck him: if he could reach the other side of island, he'd be nearer Thrum. Unable to think of any better plan, he stumbled on through the long grass, the moon high above him.

Chapter Six

Pom opened her eyes. She was very cold, her head hurt and for a moment she couldn't remember where she was. Looking round, she saw Billy peacefully sleeping beside her – and the events of the day came rushing back.

"Billy!" Pom shook him. He grunted, rolled over and sat up. "Billy, it's dark. We should be looking for the dragon."

Billy yawned, stretched and picked up the nibbled blue mushroom. "Look," he said. "Here's what made us sleep. It's magic!"

"Not a good kind of magic," Pom said

disapprovingly. "Throw it away!"

"Not yet." Billy pulled out a dirty hankie and wrapped the mushroom up.

Pom stared at him. "What are you doing that for?"

Billy put the parcel in his pocket. "I've never had anything magic before." He shook his head. "You don't get any kind of magic in an orphanage."

Pom blinked, and then, to Billy's astonishment, hugged him. "You're the nicest boy I ever met, you really are! And when we grow up, I'm going to marry you, Billy Boiler."

Bright red with embarrassment, Billy coughed to cover his confusion. "Erm … I mean … erm. Erm … should we go now?"

Pom put her arm through Billy's, and they walked on together. They hadn't gone more than a hundred steps when Pom stopped. "Listen."

Billy listened – and froze. "Something's following us!"

The two adventurers stood very still. Something was making its way towards them, moaning and squelching.

Pom squinted into the semi-darkness. "It's a boy," she whispered. "He's soaking wet … and he's crying. He hasn't seen us yet – do you think we should hide?"

"Hide? Why?" Billy spoke louder than he meant to, and the miserable Jangle heard him.

"Who's there?" he quavered.

"We are." Pom stepped forward. "This is Billy Boiler and I'm Princess Persephone Stephanie Tiffany Ja—" She paused: Billy was tugging at her arm. "What is it?"

Billy looked anxious. "You shouldn't tell people

who we are until *we* know who *they* are! It could be dangerous!"

"I don't see why," Pom said. She turned back to Jangle. "So … who are you?"

Jangle, even though he was wet, cold and thoroughly miserable, had been impressed by Pom's declaration of royal birth. The darkness hid her faded dress and tangled hair, and her voice was clear and authoritative. It reminded him of Queen Planchette and he gave a half-bow before straightening up in order to introduce himself: "Jangle, Prime Minister of Thrum!"

"THRUM?" Pom and Billy spoke together.

"Yes." Jangle was baffled by their reaction. "Why?"

Billy looked at Pom in warning, but she took no notice. "I'm from Strüggen," she said, "and I've never met anyone from Thrum before. How do you do?"

The moonlight made it difficult for Pom and Billy to see, but Jangle went pale. "Are you … *spies*?" He swallowed nervously.

"We're looking for the dragon." Pom was matter of fact. "What are you here for?"

Pom's reply made Jangle more confident. "I'm on a mission." He held out his gold chain. "Like I said: I'm the prime minister!"

Pom gave a dismissive snort and folded her arms. "We got rid of ours. Father said he was useless. So what mission are you on? Are you looking for the dragon too?"

"Atchooo!" Jangle sneezed loudly. "I'm…" He stopped to think. Surely it would be a mistake to say he had been sent to look for spy-ships from Strüggen? Perhaps it was best to be reasonably honest, and go for a half-truth. Besides, Pom and

Billy might help him get rid of Alberta. "I was just having a little look at the island, but a terrible and ferocious turtle attacked me, so I had to escape." He puffed out his chest. "It chased me for hours, but it couldn't catch me. I'm a very fast swimmer."

"Turtles don't hurt people." Pom looked superior. "Don't you know anything? We had one once in Strüggen and she used to tow us around the harbour in our rowing boats. She was a complete darling, but Father said she ate too much cake and he got rid of her. I cried for days, but he wouldn't ask her to come back. She cried too, and then she swam away, and I don't know where she went."

Jangle opened his mouth, then shut it again. What if his terrible and ferocious turtle turned out to be the same as Pom's complete darling? He decided to change the subject. "Did you say you were looking for a dragon?"

"Yes." Pom nodded. "Me and Billy, we're going to find the dragon and take it home. Why don't you come with us?"

The Prime Minister of Thrum was caught in a tangle of mixed thoughts. Would it be a good thing or a bad thing if the dragon was taken to Strüggen? Queen Planchette had said the dragon was guarding the gold … so would that mean Thrum could claim the treasure as its own?

But who did the dragon belong to? Should he immediately declare it the property of Queen Planchette? But that might make Pom and Billy leave him on his own … and that was a terrifying idea.

"I'll come with you," he said, then added, "Of course, there may not be a dragon."

"Oh yes there is!" Pom was emphatic. "The Mumble said there was one, didn't he, Billy?"

Billy took his time answering. His life in the orphanage had taught him to be suspicious when meeting someone new. He suppressed a sigh and did his best to look enthusiastic. "Yes. The Mumble said there was a dragon…"

"Oh." Jangle shivered. "Are you sure you want to find it?"

Pom had had enough. "I thought boys were supposed to be brave? If you don't want to come, just stay here." She pushed her hair out of her face and set off at a brisk trot. Billy followed her and Jangle, after a moment's hesitation, followed Billy.

"Listen!" They had been walking for twenty minutes before Pom held up her hand. "Can you hear that? It's a kind of rumbling noise … and I think it's coming from over there."

Billy strained his ears, but could hear nothing. He was, however, gradually realizing that there was a faint glow in the direction that Pom was pointing to. Jangle had seen it too, and he began to wail. "I can see fire. It's the dragon and it'll gobble us up – I know it will!"

"YES!" Pom gave a skip of triumph. "Let's hurry!" And she began to run as fast as she could. Billy, taken by surprise, was slow to run after her and Jangle clutched at him.

"Don't go! Let's go back! Even the turtle's better

than a dragon!"

Billy tried to shake himself free, but Jangle was three times his size and desperate.

"I'm scared, I'm really, REALLY scared! I want to go home."

As Billy looked at his quivering companion, he felt a stirring of sympathy. "You can go if you want," he said. "I won't hold it against you. I'm scared too, but I have to go after Pom."

"You don't! You can come back with me." And Jangle began to pull Billy back the way they had come.

"Listen!" Billy was surprised to hear himself shouting. "Either you go on your own, or you come with me – you've got to decide."

Jangle burst into noisy tears. "Don't bully me," he sobbed. "I don't like it!"

Billy sighed. "I wasn't bullying you. Now, are you coming with me or not?"

Wiping his nose with the back of his hand, Jangle gave a sullen nod. "I suppose I have to."

"Good." Billy looked round, but Pom was well out of sight.

With an anxious heart he set off towards the glow on the horizon – and Jangle, puffing hard, lumbered behind him.

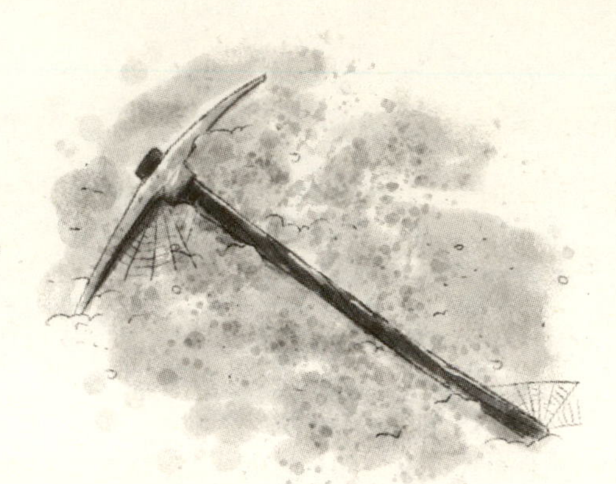

Chapter Seven

Pom had hardly noticed Billy and Jangle weren't with her. Her thoughts were an excited jumble … what would the dragon be like? The glow ahead of her was getting brighter, she was sure—

WHOOOOOSH!

She was falling. A clatter of stones accompanied her as she slipped and slid, ending up breathless on something soft and damp that squelched unpleasantly as she struggled to stand.

"**Thems be my berries!**" said a furious voice. "**Now see! Them be all squishy-squashed! You be bad, bad girlie-girl!**"

Pom rubbed her eyes. As she got used to the darkness she realized the Mumble was standing in front of her, glaring through its long seaweedy hair.

"I'm ever so sorry," Pom said, "but I didn't mean to fall down here. Can you tell me—" But the Mumble had gone, pitter-pattering into the darkness.

A faint light from the entrance above her showed Pom she was in a tunnel, hewn out of rock. Heaving herself up, she looked round. Her foot caught on something hard; bending down, she saw it was an ancient pickaxe. It was so old that the wooden handle crumbled under her touch, and the metal was thick with rust and cobwebs.

Someone hacked out this tunnel! Pom's heart beat faster. *That's so exciting! Maybe it leads to the dragon's cave? Oh – but where's Billy? I'll get out of here and find him … and then we can explore.*

This was easier said than done. The rock walls were damp and slippery, and although Pom could see the sky above her there was no way she could climb back. She tried again and again until her hands and knees were sore, but it was hopeless. She called Billy's name, but there was no answer; defeated, she sat down.

What do I do now? she asked herself. *I've got to do something – I can't stay here!* She shivered and took a deep breath. *The Mumble must be going somewhere, so I'd better go that way too—*

"Atchoo, atchoo, ATCHOO!"

As she recovered from her sneezing fit, Pom smelled smoke. For a moment it meant nothing, but then she jumped to her feet.

The dragon! I was right … she must be somewhere near! The idea that the dragon might be living in the tunnel made her stomach twist, but further thought persuaded her this was unlikely. *How would she stretch her wings? And we saw fire. She must be out in the open.*

Reassured, Pom began hurrying after the Mumble. The faint echo of smoke stayed with her, but every so often there was a gust of fresh air from somewhere ahead of her.

Is there another entrance? she thought.

Five minutes later she understood. A twist in the passage revealed a deep black hole right beside the narrow path – a hole that would be all too easy to slip into. Easing her way past, Pom peered nervously down; she could hear waves gurgling and sucking greedily at the rocks far below, but all she could see was darkness.

The Mumble was sitting on the other side sucking its paw. When it saw Pom, it glowered. "**Nasty girlie-girl did spoil berries. Now Mumble has to pick, pick, pick again! Takes long time. Makes Mumble tired.**"

Pom held out her hands in apology. "I'm really sorry. Were they for your supper?"

"**Silly girlie-girl!**" The Mumble made a face. "**Mumble eats fish, not berries!**"

"Then why were you picking them?" Pom asked.

The Mumble blinked several times, but didn't seem able to find an answer. Instead, it pulled at its hair and shuffled its feet, while Pom looked at it in surprise.

"That was a huge basket," she said. "If they weren't for you, who were they for?"

This was too much for the Mumble. It began muttering and whispering to itself – then, with a final squeak of, "**Girlie-girl mind own business!**" it held its nose and jumped into the sea hole.

Pom heard the splash as it hit the water, and

shook her head. "What did I say? I only asked who the berries were for. Oh well..."

On the other side of the hole, the passage widened, and as Pom turned the corner she saw an old and rotten bucket had been left on the ground. A couple of rusty pistols were lying a few steps further on, together with several leather bags that crumbled when Pom touched them. A faded jacket and an eyepatch were draped over a rock and a bent cutlass was abandoned behind a stone.

It looks as if there was a fight here long ago, Pom thought. *Maybe it was Pirate Jed Josiah Jones and his crew? Oh no! Looks like the dragon had them for breakfast.*

This made her pause for a moment. A dragon that was willing to take on a group of pirates was hardly likely to be the domestic type that she could take home to show her father.

Pom bit her lip, then straightened her shoulders and marched on. *I'm Persephone Stephanie Tiffany Jane, and I'm not scared of anything!*

And she tried to ignore the fluttering in her stomach.

By the time she finally emerged from the tunnel, Pom felt calmer. In front of her was a small open space, a natural arena surrounded by craggy rock walls that soared up to the night sky above. Opposite was a dark cavernous opening. Pom looked at it in wonder.

Could that be the dragon's cave? It looks as if it ought to be … but there isn't any smoke and there aren't any bones lying around. I'm sure there ought to be bones. Oh, I do wish Billy was here!

Glancing up at the sky, she saw it was just beginning to get light.

Do dragons sleep at night? If I tiptoe over to the cave entrance I could look inside … and if there is a dragon, I can creep away again before it wakes up. Pom made her decision.

I'm going to try!

Chapter Eight

Billy and Jangle were making slow progress. Jangle complained about his feet, his knees and his stomach; Billy did his best to encourage his companion, but he was beginning to wish he had let him go back to his boat.

He wasn't even certain they were going in the right direction – there was now no glow in the sky to guide them and Pom had left no tracks. The moon shone intermittently between heavy clouds and from time to time he caught a glimpse of a star, but at other times the night sky was dark. He and Jangle tripped over roots, bumped themselves on rocks and were clutched at by thorny bushes. There was no path.

"I can't go another step!" Jangle announced suddenly. "I'm staying here till it's morning. I'm absolutely exhausted and I'm going to go to sleep – so there!" And he threw himself down onto a bed of bracken.

Two seconds later, he was snoring loudly.

Billy sighed. He was hot and sweaty and tired too, but he was desperate to find Pom. What if she was in trouble?

A small breeze sprang up, and Billy turned to face it – and was rewarded with a faint smell of smoke. Immediately hope leapt up again.

It's that way! he told himself. *If I head towards that little hill I'll be going in the right direction…* He bent down and shook Jangle, but there was no response. For a moment Billy dithered. Should he go, or should he stay? *I'll go as far as the little hill. I might be able to see more from there. And then I'll come back and get Jangle.*

By the time he reached the top of the hill, Billy was panting hard. He had had to climb the last few yards on his hands and knees – the hill was small but steep, and it was all he could do not to cry out. The ridge at the summit hid a small circular chasm, making the hill into something very like a chimney.

Clutching at a twisted gorse bush for safety, Billy peered down. Below he could just make out an open space; as he looked, a small figure came into view … and his heart missed a beat.

Pom! He was certain it was Pom. But what was she doing? She was walking slowly – no. She was tiptoeing. In his anxiety to see he leant too far forward: a shower of small stones broke away from the edge and fell. Billy drew back sharply and, holding his breath, listened intently.

There was no shout from below. Only silence.

Billy counted to ten before he crept back and, as he did so, realized he could see more clearly. Daybreak wasn't far away; the clouds on the eastern horizon were growing lighter.

Encouraged, he peered over the edge again. With a start, Billy realized that what he had taken to be a dark shadow was the entrance to a cave and, as he stared, a small puff of smoke floated out.

There was no sign of Pom.

Chapter Nine

King Vigor of Strüggen was woken by a loud and determined knocking on the front door of the palace. He opened his eyes and squinted at the window. It was hardly light and he was at the point of deciding he had been dreaming, when the knocking began again.

The king sat up with a start. "Thrum! They're invading us!" and he jumped out of bed. Before he could find his shoes the door opened, and the queen came hurrying in.

"My dear," she said, "there's a horrid fisherman here and he won't go away. He says he wants

his boat back right now this minute, because he always goes fishing early in the morning … and, Vigor – he says it was Persephone who took it!"

"Nonsense." King Vigor wrapped his dressing gown more tightly round his pyjama-clad body. "Ridiculous. Rubbish. The very idea! Throw him in the dungeons."

"Whatever you say, dear," the queen said. "But Vigor, I think he might be right. Persephone's bed hasn't been slept in."

"What?" The king stared at his wife. "What do you mean?"

The door opened again as Prince Dribble came stomping in. "Pom's a naughty, naughty girl! She isn't in bed."

"You see, Vigor?" the queen said. "Our daughter is missing."

King Vigor shook his head. "She'll be in the kitchen with Cook."

Dribble climbed onto the bed. "She's not in the kitchen, 'cos I looked. I wanted biscuits … and I want a biscuit now. Get me a biscuit!"

The queen patted his head. "In a minute, sweetie pie." She turned to the king. "The fisherman says Persephone was with a boy and they were going to Bullion Island."

"Bullion Island?" The king's eyes popped. "Call the captains! Prepare the ships! We must fetch her back."

Queen Hyacinth went pale. "But what about the dragon?"

King Vigor paused for a moment. "The dragon … ah. Yes. I know! We'll fly a white flag to show we come in peace."

"But will the dragon understand about white flags, my dear?" the queen asked anxiously.

The king puffed out his chest. "Only one way to find out."

Prince Dribble had been listening with interest, and he pulled at his mother's arm. "Want to see a dragon!"

"No, precious one," his mother said. "It's not safe—"

"WAAAAAAAH!" Dribble went purple and began to roar. Queen Hyacinth tried to hug him, but he pushed her away. "WANT TO SEE A DRAGON!"

"Hush, hush … of course you can, my little poppet." The queen made soothing noises. "We'll all go on the pretty boat and see the dragon, won't we, Daddy?"

King Vigor opened his mouth to say *Absolutely not!* But seeing his wife's expression, he changed his mind. "Yes, dear."

Far away in Thrum, Queen Planchette was striding up and down the quayside. "Everything ready?"

The captain saluted. "Almost, Your Majesty. Just waiting for the flag, Your Majesty." A faintly disapproving look crossed his face. "Are you quite sure you want to fly a white flag, Your Majesty?"

"Quite sure." The queen was firm. "We're off to see what's happened to the Prime Minister of Thrum, Hastings. He didn't come back last night, and that's a young man who loves his food and his bed." She sighed. "Strüggen are sure to notice our ships and we don't want to blunder into a war by mistake."

The captain saluted again. "Just as you say, Your Majesty. And … erm… The men asked me to ask you … should we load the cannons?"

"Load the cannons?" Planchette raised her eyebrows. "Certainly not. This is a peaceful mission."

"But … what about the dragon?"

"We don't need to worry about that," Planchette said. "If I know our prime minister, which I do, he'll be shivering somewhere on the shoreline. He'd never dare go inland and stir up anything scary. We'll swoop round, pick him up and get back here as fast as we can."

"Just as you say, Your Majesty." The captain didn't sound convinced, but he saluted a third time and marched away.

Planchette settled her crown more firmly on her head, and stepped onto the deck of the flagship.

Chapter Ten

"Well, well, well. Slither my scales and tickle my ancient whiskers! If I'm not much mistaken – and Angelina is NEVER mistaken – it's a girl! A girl, creeping into my cave without so much as a please or an excuse me."

It was a dusty, rusty voice that sounded as if it hadn't been used for a very long time, and it came from somewhere over Pom's head.

Pom jumped and looked round. All she could see was cold hard rock on either side and pitch black darkness above; she had been certain the cave was empty.

"Hello!" she called. "Where are you?"

There was a small puff of greenish smoke that made her cough, then a rumbling sound followed by a wheeze. "Darling heart, I can't possibly come out yet. It's much too early. An old lady needs her beauty sleep. So – let's have a little chat instead. What, exactly, are you doing here?"

Pom's stomach began to flutter; she tried to ignore it, but it wasn't easy. "I wanted to see a dragon," she said. "Erm. You *are* a dragon, aren't you?"

"Oh yes, my sweet child. I'm very much a dragon." There was another puff of smoke. "But are you really here to look at me? Or, dear thing, might you, just possibly, be here for … the gold?"

Despite the friendliness of the words, there was a subtle menace in Angelina's tone and for a brief moment Pom wondered if she should make her escape while she had the chance. She swallowed hard while her thoughts raced.

Come on, Pom. Don't be such a scaredy-cat! she told herself.

"Actually," she said, and she took a step forward to prove she wasn't frightened, "I don't much care for gold. It makes people greedy."

An approving snort came from the darkness over her head. "Quite right, precious girl. It brings out the worst in people. Does them no good at all! But we dragons know how to look after it. We love it for itself, you see, not for what it can buy. It's the look of it we love, the feel, the sound, the taste, the smell… So very, very wonderful. Glittering, gleaming, glistening gold, heaped in piles, tumbling out of boxes, scattered around… Beautiful, beautiful shining shimmering gold…"

Her voice had softened to a low croon, but Pom was thinking too hard to notice.

"I know Father's very keen on gold," said Pom. "He likes it much more than he likes me. He's the king of Strüggen, you see – and the people of Thrum like it too. Father says they want Pirate Jones' treasure all for themselves, and he's got loads of warships ready to fight them." She paused as she remembered Billy asking why the kingdoms couldn't share. "Father wants it all for Strüggen."

"And THAT, my poppet, is why I stay here wearing myself to a shadow. Puffing out smoke takes effort, you know – but it has to be done." Angelina wheezed a chuckle. "I need to remind those warmongering greedy kingdoms that I exist, so they don't come bothering me."

Pom nodded. "Everyone knows stories about dragons and how dangerous they are."

"Really?" Angelina chuckled again. "Excellent! But in all seriousness, my little friend, do you see how important I am? If it wasn't for me, Thrum and Strüggen would immediately start fighting each other … all for that glorious, glimmering, glistening gold."

"Oh." Pom leant against the rock wall. "So in fact, you're doing a good deed by being here."

"Correct, dear child! How extremely perceptive you are. It's a positive pleasure talking to you."

Pom sighed. "I do wish I could see you."

There was a slithering noise, a blast of hot smoky air – and an old, old dragon dropped down in front of Pom from somewhere high above. Her scarlet wings were tattered and faded, but her long sinuous body was covered in silver scales that glittered and shone.

Pom was wide eyed. "WOW!" she said breathlessly. "WOW! You're... You're AMAZING!"

Angelina bowed and smiled. "So kind." She paused. "Did nobody ever tell you it was rude to stare, dearest child?"

"I'm sorry," Pom apologized. "I couldn't help noticing you were wearing spectacles. I somehow never thought a dragon would wear spectacles."

"Is that so, dear?" Angelina's smile was now a little forced. "Fancy!"

Aware that she had been tactless, Pom decided to change the subject. "Look, it's light outside! It's been lovely meeting you, but I'd better be going."

"Oh no, darling heart." Angelina shook her head and slithered past Pom, so her huge silvery body blocked the entrance to the cave. "I'm so dreadfully sorry, but now you're here, you have to stay. But don't worry. We'll have lovely conversations about all kinds of things. It'll be huge fun."

"Stay here?" Pom's legs turned to jelly. "But I can't. I can't possibly stay here!" A terrible thought came to her. "Are you going to EAT me?"

"EAT you?" Angelina shook with wheezy laughter and the cave filled with smoke. "You'd give me dreadful indigestion, darling!"

Pom blinked. "Indigestion?" A thought came to her. "Goodness! You're not vegetarian, are you?"

Angelica looked surprised. "What a clever little thing you are, dear child. Of course I am. If I was the usual sort of dragon, you'd have been gobbled and chomped long ago."

Pom clenched her fists to stop herself from trembling. "A vegetarian dragon? Well, that's good news." She hoped she sounded more cheerful than she felt. "But I still don't see why you want to keep me here – especially if you're not going to eat me."

"Think, darling, think!" Angelina looked pained. "If you leave here, people will guess my little secret … and how scary is an ancient vegetarian dragon who believes in peace, love and harmony? Strüggen and Thrum would be here in no time. They'd come raging in with swords and knives and all kinds of horrid nasty things and take away the gold. My precious, precious shining heaps of gold. Oh, if only I could hide it away where no one could ever find it – nobody except ME!" Her voice had grown more and more hysterical, and Pom drew back in alarm. "No. You must stay here. I can't let you go."

And before Pom could say another word the dragon stretched out a long scaly arm, picked her up and tossed her onto a ledge, hidden high in the darkness of the cave.

"There – I'll share my sleeping platform with you, dearest child. So be grateful: be very, very grateful..."

Chapter Eleven

Billy was sitting at the bottom of the hill, his thoughts whirling round and round.

A growling noise made him jump up. The nearest bramble bush was shaking; as Billy anxiously watched, a greenish grey head emerged from under the lowest branches.

"**Urrrrrrr,**" it said.

"Mumble!" Billy gasped with relief. "I'm so pleased it's you!"

"**Urrrrrrr.**" The growl was friendly and the Mumble held up a paw in greeting. "**Where girlie-girl?**"

Billy pointed to the top of the hill. "I saw her walk towards the dragon's cave, but she hasn't come out again. Oh, Mumble, I don't know what to do."

The Mumble put its head on one side. "**Mumble telled you go home.**"

"But what about the dragon?" Billy wanted to know. "Will it eat her?"

"**No danger from dragon.**" The Mumble scuttled closer. "**Never, never tell, but dragon don't eat nothing but berries.**"

"Berries?" Billy's eyes opened wide. "Are you sure?"

The Mumble nodded. "**Us brings berries every day. Us brings berries, dragon lets us stay. Secret! Shh! Never, never tell. Promise?**"

Billy drew his finger across his throat. "Strike me dead if I whisper a word. But … what's the dragon going to do with Pom?"

If the Mumble had had any shoulders it would have shrugged. As it was, it held out its paws to show its lack of ideas. "**Us don't know. Go see?**"

"What?" Billy stared. "How can we go and see?"

"**Mumble has secret tunnel. Nobody knows but Mumble! Follow,**" the Mumble ordered, and it scurried towards the bramble bush. A moment later it vanished.

Crawling after it, Billy found a well-hidden tunnel entrance; taking a deep breath, he wriggled after his guide.

At first the walls of the tunnel pressed so tightly that Billy wondered if he was going to get stuck, but gradually they widened and he was able to move more easily. He also became aware that there were other tunnels branching off, and the scary thought came to him that if the Mumble disappeared he would be lost underground for ever.

"**Tippy-toe!**" The Mumble's voice broke into Billy's thoughts. "**Cave. Upstand!**"

Billy was able to get to his feet. "Is it much further?" he whispered.

"**Looky see.**" The Mumble took Billy's hand in its scaly paw and, as it led him round a corner,

Billy gasped. In front of him was a narrow opening between two enormous rocks; a faint light was filtering through – light, heat and a wisp of green smoke.

"What—" he began, but the Mumble stepped heavily on his foot.

"**Quietness,**" it hissed. "**Looky see. Is peepy hole: see dragon's sleeping place.**"

Billy scrambled forward. Hardly daring to breathe, he peered through the opening.

An eye was looking back at him.

"Billy? Billy, is that you?" The voice was wonderfully familiar and Billy began to breathe again.

"Pom! Are you okay?"

"Well … sort of." There was a muffled sound that sounded as if it might be a suppressed sob before Pom went on. "I'm stuck on a ledge and I can't get down. The dragon wants to keep me here. She says she can't let me go, or people will know she isn't actually at all fierce and *then* they'll take away her gold. Oh, Billy … you've absolutely got to think of an idea to help me escape. I can't stay here for ever, I can't!"

On the other side of the rocks, Billy studied the narrow gap to see if Pom could squeeze through.

But there had to be another way. "Is the dragon there now?"

"She's outside," Pom told him. "She's doing her exercises, and breathing smoke in case there's anyone looking for me. Have you had an idea yet?"

Billy hadn't – and he wasn't sure he ever would. The darkness of the cave was pressing down on him and the smoke that drifted round him was making his eyes water. "What's the dragon like?"

Pom considered. "She's called Angelina and she's mad about gold. She keeps on and on and ON talking about it."

"Have you seen any?" Billy wanted to know.

"No, but it must be very near here. She wouldn't want to be far away from it."

A small scaly paw pulled at Billy's arm. "**Gold in dragon's cave**," the Mumble said.

"**Is all there!**" The paw pointed to the gap. "**Other end. Lots, lots gold.**"

"Billy, who are you talking to?" Pom sounded anxious.

Billy came closer to the gap between them. "It's the Mumble. He says the gold's on the shelf where you're sitting."

"What?" There was the sound of scrabbling, and then Pom said, "Oh, I think I've found it. There's goblets and crowns and plates and all sorts here! And— Shh … she's coming back."

There was the sound of heavy leather wings flapping and folding, and the *scratch-scratch* of sharp claws on rocky floor. From his hiding place, Billy couldn't see the dragon, but the air grew warmer and a curl of smoke drifted up. With sudden alarm, he realized he was about to sneeze; he clapped his hands over his mouth, but it was no good.

"ATCHOOO!"

"Oh, excuse me! I'm so sorry!" It was Pom,

and Billy sighed with relief at her quick thinking. From below came a rusty snort of laughter.

"Darling girl, you'll have to get used to the smoke. We're going to be close companions for a long, long time, you know." Pom didn't answer and Angelina went on, "But I've had such a clever idea. We don't want you getting bored, do we? So I'm going to put you to work. My glorious gold is spread higgledy-piggledy here and there, and I fear it might not be safe." The elderly voice deepened into a gloating purr. "My shining, gleaming, golden gold... My glorious, glistening gold... My precious, precious, PRECIOUS—"

"So what do you want me to do, exactly?" Pom's voice broke across the dragon's. "Do you want me to count it?"

"Oh no, dear heart." There was a rustling noise and Billy, cramped and uncomfortable in his hiding place, wondered what the dragon could be doing. A moment later he heard her say, "Here you are, sweet one – catch! Have you got it? It's an old fishing net. You can make it into a wonderfully big bag, and I'll fill it with gold... I can keep the bag safe, for ever and ever and ever."

Billy squeezed nearer to the gap and caught a glimpse of Pom. She was holding a large net and, as he looked, she turned a despairing face towards him. Angelina's voice echoed up from below.

"And now I'm going to have a little snooze. Time to start working, petal... Enjoy!" And a moment later there was the sound of steady snoring.

"Billy! Are you still there?" Pom was whispering so softly Billy had to strain his ears to hear her.

"I'm here," he said.

"Have you had any ideas yet? Is there some way I can get to where you are?"

Billy looked at the solid walls of rock. "I don't think so," he said. "We'll have to get you out another way."

"Another way?" Pom sounded suddenly hopeful. "Is there another tunnel?"

"Hang on, I'll ask the Mumble." Billy eased himself out of his crevice and into the main tunnel.

The Mumble was sitting on the floor scratching itself; before Billy could even ask his question it shook its head. "**Only tunnel to here. Us brings berries this way! Berries for dragon.**" It put its head on one side. "**Boy help Mumble? Pick berries? Naughty girlie-girl did squish-squash basket of berries and dragon be hungry soon. Always hungry after sleeping...**"

Sleep! A sudden idea flooded Billy's mind with hope. He still had the remains of the blue mushroom in his pocket; if he could mix it with berries, the dragon would surely fall into a sleep so deep that they could find a way to escape. He wriggled back to the gap and whispered, "Pom, I've had an idea. I'll be back as soon as I can!"

A scaly hand pulled at his arm. "**Us must go find berries now,**" said the Mumble.

Billy nodded. "I'm coming with you."

Chapter Twelve

The cave felt even darker and more unpleasant when Pom knew she was alone with the sleeping dragon. She had no idea how to make any kind of bag from the fishing net draped over her knees, and only Billy's promise that he had had an idea gave her any hope.

She crawled a little way along her shelf, being careful not to make any noise, and found it widened more and more the further she went. It also grew darker. She began to feel her way with one hand held out in front of her and, after only a short while, was brought to a halt.

Her way was blocked … but by what? Pom gave a tentative push – and there was a sudden crash and clatter as a number of metal objects cascaded off the shelf. At once there was a terrifying roar from below, and a blast of heat that sent Pom cowering against the rock face.

"I'm so sorry," she called. "I was just trying to find a bit more space so I could make the bag."

Pom's voice faded as Angelina's head rose up beside her. The dragon's eyes were blazing behind her spectacles and Pom felt her heart begin to pound as Angelina hissed, "You must never, ever, ever do that again!"

"I really am sorry…" Pom was annoyed to hear that her voice was trembling. She bit her lip and told herself that princesses were meant to be brave. "It was an accident. I'll pick it all up, but you'll need to help me down first. It's too far to jump."

Angelina snorted and a cloud of smoke surrounded Pom, making her cough and splutter. "Oh no, no, no, darling! You think you can slip away when I'm not looking, don't you? But it won't work: you're here to stay, my little chicken. So get used to it." She drew back a little and inspected her prisoner. "Just be grateful I believe in peace, love and harmony. My grandfather would have swallowed you up in one gulp. A dragon's hoard is their most precious possession … always remember that! Now, wriggle back to where you were and let me sleep."

Pom did as she was told, but she was thoughtful as she edged her way along, still clutching the net. The Mumble had been right; the pirate's hoard was stacked at the end of her shelf. And then, with an unpleasant jolt, she remembered that her father wanted it for himself.

Thrum as well, she thought. *And Angelina loves it more than anyone. What a horrible thing gold is! I wish I could throw it all away…*

Had she had an idea? Pom leant back against the cave wall in order to think things out.

If there wasn't any gold, Angelina wouldn't have anything to guard – so she'd have to let me go home. She began to feel excited. *And when I tell Father there isn't any treasure, he'll get rid of his warships and stop worrying about Thrum, because there won't be anything to fight over. Maybe we could even be friends with them?*

Pom gave herself an enthusiastic thumbs up.

Just wait until I tell Billy he's not the only *one who has ideas!*

This thought pleased her so much that she almost let the fishing net slip; only a last minute grab saved it, and she hauled it back. As she did so, she looked at it properly for the first time.

It's like Cook's string shopping bag, she told herself. *Maybe I can make something after all? And then we can put the gold inside and haul it away— OH NO!* Her excitement vanished like a popped bubble as she realized the foolishness of this idea. *But we'll never be able to do that without Angelina seeing what we're doing. Maybe it wasn't such a clever plan after all…*

And Pom drooped over her net.

"Pom?" The whisper was right beside her ear. "It's me, Billy – and I've got a plan. Well, sort of. Is the dragon still asleep?"

Pom nodded, then realized Billy couldn't see her from his limited view point. "Yes. Oh, Billy! I thought I'd had SUCH a good idea and I was going to boast about how good it was. Then I realized it was rubbish!"

Billy, tucked uncomfortably in the narrow space between the rocks, heard the disappointment in Pom's voice. "I bet it wasn't rubbish," he said encouragingly. "What was it?"

With a sigh, Pom explained her idea of bagging up the gold in the fishing net and throwing it into the sea. "But we'd never ever get it out of here," she said. "How could we get it past Angelina? I told you it was a rubbish idea."

She waited hopefully for Billy to tell her it was very nearly a good idea, but he said nothing. The silence grew longer and Pom began to feel anxious. Did he think she was so stupid that he couldn't say anything? She knelt up to peer through the gap, and saw Billy was staring into space. "Billy? What is it?"

"It's not rubbish," Billy said. "I really, REALLY like the idea of getting rid of the gold... But we need to rescue you first. The Mumble's here with a basket of berries for the dragon – and I've mixed in the blue mushroom. I just hope it doesn't taste weird—"

He was interrupted by a loud snort and a plume of greenish smoke. Angelina had woken up.

"Darling!" she called. "Sweet thing! I'm so terribly, TERRIBLY hungry. Is there any sign of a strange, furry little creature bringing me some delicious berries? There's a little gap in the rocks behind you. Have a tiny peep and see if it's there."

"I'll have a look," Pom said. She turned round and mouthed at Billy, *What do I say?*

"Say yes," Billy whispered, his voice a mere breath. "And pretend you're scared..."

"Yes," Pom said, loudly and clearly – then added, "Ooooh, it's all hairy! Will it hurt me?"

Angelina, with a flap of her wings, arrived on the ledge beside Pom. She was licking her lips and her eyes gleamed greedily. "Hurt you? It can't reach." She crouched down beside the opening. "Feed me!" she ordered. "Feed me NOW!"

The Mumble, on the other side of the rocks, carefully tipped the basket of berries so they fell through the gap and into Angelina's open mouth. The dragon made no comment about the taste; all she said was, "More!"

It was only when the basket was completely empty that she gave a loud burp. "Excellent!" she said. "A fine crop."

Billy, hidden behind the Mumble, was holding his breath. Would the mushroom work? What if it didn't? He had no alternative plan – and, so far, it appeared to have had no effect on Angelina. She was picking her teeth with a claw and spitting out pips. As she spat out the last one, she swung her heavy head round and stared at Pom.

"And how's my little helper getting on?" she asked. "Is my bag nearly finished?"

"Nearly," Pom lied. "I'd get on faster if I could see better. It's lighter on the cave floor… Could you help me down?"

"No! Stay there!" Billy, forgetting where he was, had spoken out loud.

Angelina's nostrils flared and she reared up to see where the voice was coming from. Pom froze, and Billy fell backwards as the Mumble pulled him out of the way.

"**We is here, Mrs Dragon**," it said, but Angelina ignored it.

She took a deep breath. "An intruder, I heard him! Smoke… I'll smoke him out." And then, as thick green smoke began to pour out of her nostrils, she gave a sudden gasp and collapsed. A moment later heavy snores echoed round the smoke filled cave.

Pom rubbed her smarting eyes and coughed. "Angelina?" she whispered – and then again,

"ANGELINA!"

There was no response. The blue mushroom had done its work: the dragon was so fast asleep that when Pom, greatly daring, pulled at her ear, she didn't stir.

"Billy! She's asleep!"

"Good," Billy said. "My plan's working! And now, can you push the gold onto the floor?"

Pom needed no further encouragement. She wriggled along the shelf and began heaving the treasure onto the floor below; it crashed down in shining heaps and lay in a gleaming pile.

Billy watched, wishing he could help. He gave a frustrated push at the rock blocking his way. It didn't move … but was there a crack? It was too dark to see for certain.

Bending down, Billy picked up a large stone and hit the rock as hard as he could; there was a thud and a chunk fell off, leaving the gap a little wider. Billy's heart leapt – could he climb through? Was it wide enough?

He turned to the Mumble, who was picking leaves out of its long greenish hair. "Please could you push me?"

The Mumble put a scaly paw on Billy's arm. "**Boy safe here. Stay!**"

"I can't," Billy told him. "I've got to help Pom." He looked at the gap again. It seemed to get smaller and smaller as he looked, but he shook his head at the thought of giving up. *I've got to try. It's a good thing they never fed us at the orphanage…* And he began to squirm his way through.

Chapter Thirteen

Years of living on thin watery porridge had left Billy so thin that he could hide behind a gatepost, but even so it took several hefty pushes from the Mumble before he was through the gap. His ribs were bruised and aching, and there had been a bad moment when he hadn't been able to move either forwards or backwards … but a final push landed him safely on the rocky shelf beside the snoring dragon.

"Hello, Pom," he said. "I've come to help." And to his astonishment Pom flung her arms round him.

"I'm SO glad you've come," she said.

Billy, scarlet with embarrassment from the top of his head to the tip of his toes, nervously patted Pom's back. "We'll be out of here in no time," he promised, hoping this was true. "Let's get the rest of the gold off the shelf and into the net."

Pom nodded, then paused. "But Billy – how are we going to get down? We're too high to jump. The floor looks sandy, but it's solid rock."

"The net." Billy pulled it towards him. "If we hook one end onto something, we can climb down." He looked round, but could see nothing suitable. "Ummm," he said.

And then, holding his breath, he leant over Angelina's enormous head and hooked the net over the spikes on her back. She didn't stir and her snoring continued.

"Billy!" Pom was wide eyed. "What if she wakes up?"

"**No wakey-wakey for long, long, long time.**" The Mumble gave a dark chuckle, oozing his way between the rocks as if he had no bones in his body. "**Blue mushroom very strong. Boy is clever.**"

"Mumble, could you unhook the net when we reach the ground?" Billy asked, and the Mumble chuckled again.

"**Mumble help,**" he announced. "**We been thinking. Get gold gone, dragon can leave cave and find own berries. Mumble have peaceful life. Is good.**"

It was easy for Billy and Pom to climb down the net. The Mumble unhooked it and Pom spread it out on the floor. Then she and Billy began to fill it with the treasure, while the Mumble watched.

It was back-breaking work, and when at last the net was full both Billy and Pom were exhausted.

"There's an awful lot," Pom said wearily. "Can we have a rest now? I'm worn—"

Billy interrupted her. "Listen!"

Pom listened. "I can't hear anything."

"Exactly." Billy was pale. "The snoring, it's stopped!"

"Oh no…" Pom grabbed hold of the heavy net. "We've got to hurry!"

Billy was still listening. "*Shh* – no, I think it's okay. She's snoring again." He took the other side of the net and heaved. "WOW! This weighs a ton."

Pom put on what Billy privately thought of as her princessy face. "Billy, we need to work together. I'll count to three and then we'll pull. Ready? One, two, three—"

They pulled and heaved and pulled again … but the net hardly moved. Billy was breathless and Pom's face was scarlet. "It's no good," she puffed.

"We can't move it. Oh, Billy! We'll have to leave it here."

Billy wiped his face. "But you don't want to, do you?"

Pom's eyes were full of tears. "I SO want to get rid of the beastly stuff, but we can't!"

Billy scratched his head. "We might be able to do it if Jangle helped us."

"Jangle? But he'd never help us get rid of a load of gold!" Pom was horrified. "He'd think we were completely and utterly mad."

"We won't tell him." Billy looked round. "We'll say it's – it's stones."

"STONES?" Pom stared at him. "Why on earth would we throw away stones?"

"Mmmmm..." Billy racked his brains. "I know! We're blocking the dragon's secret escape route."

Pom still looked doubtful.

"It's our only chance," Billy told her. "If you want to get rid of the gold—"

"I do. I really do!" Pom was emphatic.

"—then we have to get Jangle to help," Billy told her. "But he's much too big to come the way I did. How did you get here? Could he come that way too?"

"Billy!" Pom's face broke into a smile. "You're a genius. I came through a tunnel... Look, over there on the other side." She pointed across the cave. "But have we got time?"

Billy shrugged. "I don't know. Let's hope so!"

Together they raced out of the cave, across the open space and into the tunnel. It took a moment for their eyes to adjust to the darkness – but then they were off again, Pom leading the way.

As the path narrowed beside the chasm, Billy shuddered. The black hole was a hungry mouth, the edges treacherously slippery.

"That's horrible," he said. "Imagine falling in! You'd never be seen again."

Pom clutched his arm. "You're right. So that's where we'll dump the gold... Oh, come on! Hurry, Billy, hurry!"

By the time they reached the basket of squashed berries that marked the spot where Pom had fallen into the tunnel, they were both panting. "I couldn't get out by myself," Pom puffed. "I tried and tried – but you're taller than me."

"Climb on my shoulders," Billy said. "You'll be tall enough then."

Pom didn't have enough breath to argue. She did as she was told – and then was out in the sunshine, blinking and rubbing her eyes.

Moments later Billy, with a jump and a clutch at an obliging root, was beside her. "Now to find Jangle…"

They didn't have to look far. There was a plaintive cry and then the Prime Minister of Thrum came stumbling towards them.

"You left me," he said accusingly. "You left me all alone! I might have been eaten by a monster."

"Never mind monsters," Pom said. "We need your help!"

Jangle immediately looked suspicious. "What kind of help?"

Coaxing Jangle to come with them took much longer than Pom and Billy had hoped. He wanted to go straight to the boat; he thought the idea of blocking a secret escape route was a stupid waste of time.

Pom tried flattery – "You'll be remembered for ever. I'll make sure you get a medal!" – and every kind of persuasion she could think of, but nothing worked.

Billy, seeing Pom growing redder and redder, and more and more desperate, took a deep breath. "If you don't help us, Mr Prime Minister Jangle, we'll leave you here." He folded his arms and did his best to look fierce. "We can run faster than you, you know we can. We'll take the boats and we'll leave you here all alone … and sooner or later the dragon will wake up and find you. But if you help us, I absolutely *promise* we'll take you safely back to Thrum."

Jangle stared at him, his lower lip trembling.

"Billy's right," Pom said. "And I promise too. You have the solemn word of Princess Persephone Stephanie—"

"Okay." Jangle, green with terror, nodded furiously. "Okay, okay. I'll do it."

There was another tense discussion when Jangle discovered he was expected to lower himself into what he considered an earthy grave.

"I can't go in there!" he wailed. "I can't."

"Oh, for heaven's sake." Pom, frustrated by the delay, ran at him and pushed him hard. Taken by surprise he wobbled, shrieked and fell into the hole. There was a terrified yell – then sudden silence.

Pom and Billy hastily slid after him, and were astonished to find him calmly eating berries.

"Food at last," he announced. "I was starving."

"Bring them with you," Billy said. "We've got to get moving."

Jangle picked up the basket and peered at the berries. "They're a bit squashed, but I don't mind."

"Come on," Pom urged and she set off at a trot.

Billy grabbed Jangle's arm and marched him after her. As long as the prime minister was allowed to keep eating, they made reasonable progress. Billy was worried the sea hole would cause a problem, but Jangle hardly seemed to notice it. He was much more concerned that the berries were almost finished.

"Oh, PLEASE hurry!" Pom begged. "The sooner we get there, the sooner we can get away… And then we can go home."

Chapter Fourteen

Much to Pom and Billy's relief, Angelina was still snoring when they got back to the cave.

Jangle, twitching at her every breath, hesitated in the cave entrance. "She's waking up! I'm sure she's waking up!"

"Then we need to hurry," Pom told him. "I'll count to three and then we'll rush in and grab the net. Are you ready?"

Unwillingly Jangle nodded and Pom counted: "One, two, three – NOW!"

Fear gave Jangle extra strength, and the three of them were able to haul the net out of the cave and across the open space outside. Once in the tunnel they dragged it as fast as they could go, Jangle muttering, "Faster, faster..."

By the time they reached the sea hole he was puffing and sweating, and as they dropped the heavy net beside it he heaved a sigh of relief.

Pom eyes were shining. "We've done it! Push the – erm – stones over. Ready? One, two, *three*!"

There was a mighty *SPLASH* and Pirate Jed Josiah Jones' gold was gone. At that exact moment, the tunnel filled with choking greenish smoke.

Angelina had woken up.

Billy grabbed Pom's hand and seized Jangle's wrist. "RUN!" he shouted and the three of them hurtled along the tunnel. An ear-splitting roar from behind made them run even faster, though their feet felt like lead and their hearts were pounding.

On and on and *on* they ran, until at last they managed to scramble out into the fresh air. For a brief moment they stopped to wipe their streaming eyes and catch their breath, and as they did so a bramble bush quivered and the Mumble popped out.

"**We is here,**" it said. "**Hurry! Boy want boatie-boat?**"

"YES!" Billy said, and the Mumble nodded and set off at an unexpectedly speedy trot. Pom and Billy raced after him and Jangle, after a terrified look over his shoulder at the waves of smoke billowing out from the tunnel, ran too.

Finally, they saw it: the Dillyman Sea, sparkling in the sunshine.

By the time they reached the bay where the boat was hidden, Jangle was purple in the face and panting. Once he was on the sand he collapsed, gasping.

"Take me home! You promised! Take me home NOW!"

Pom took no notice; she and Billy were frantically hauling the boat down to the water. When Jangle saw what they were doing he leapt to his feet, dashed after them and flung himself on top of the oars.

"You can't go without me. You can't!"

"We weren't going to," Pom said crossly. "Get off the oars and help us."

Jangle didn't answer. His eyes were bulging as he pointed a quivering finger towards the island. Billy and Pom turned to look, and they too stared.

Angelina was hurling herself down the rocky cliff, half-flying, half-sliding, and smoke was pouring from her flaring nostrils.

"Stop!" she roared. "Stop!"

"Oh no … she's coming after us," Jangle quavered, "and she's going to gobble us up!"

Pom didn't argue with him. The loss of Angelina's gold might well have made the dragon forget all about peace, love and vegetarianism. She grabbed an oar as a weapon, but as Angelina surged down the beach towards her she dropped it and stood up very straight.

"Always face your enemy," she muttered.

Billy nodded and took his place beside her,

hoping nobody would notice he was shaking. Jangle cowered down at the bottom of the boat and hid his head in a rusty bucket, and the Mumble scurried away.

Angelina skidded to a halt and took a deep breath.

We're going to be frizzled, Pom told herself, *I'm sure we are.* She held Billy's hand tightly as she shut her eyes and waited for the burst of flame.

Nothing happened.

Pom opened her eyes. Angelina was sitting on the sand in front of her, looking extraordinarily pleased with herself.

"Darling precious girl," she said, "do introduce me to this delightful young man! Your rescuer, I imagine? That sniveling wretch in the boat is hardly made from the stuff of heroes."

Pom blinked and looked at Billy. "What's happened to her? Why isn't she angry?"

Angelina twitched her ears. "What was that, my precious?"

"We threw away your treasure," Pom said. "We thought… We thought you'd be angry!"

"Angry?" Angelina looked astonished. "But it's not gone, has it? You hid it, deep in the sea hole."

Billy stared at her. "But how did you know it was there?"

Angelina put her head to one side. "Dragons can smell gold, you know, even under water. You're very, *very* clever, dear hearts. No one from Thrum will find it now, nor anyone from Strüggen. It's hidden from everyone – everyone except ME! Such a joy, my darlings. I can dive into the sea and have a loving little gaze at it any time I want, but I won't need to guard it day and night, night and day … so I'm free. Free, free, FREE!"

She blew a smoke ring towards Pom, making her cough.

"I hope you realize, you dear sweet thing, that you and your handsome friend have changed my life. If there's anything I can do for either of you, anything at all – do say."

Pom's mind was whirling as she tried to take in Angelina's words; it was Billy who said, "Excuse me for asking, but can you fly?"

The dragon thought for a moment, then shook her head. "I wouldn't care to try a long journey, dear boy. It's been over a hundred years since I settled in that cave." She stretched out her wide leathery wings, and Billy saw they were faded and tattered at the edges. "But let's see, shall we?"

And next minute Angelina was in the air. Up and up she flew … and then she was falling, only just managing to right herself before she landed with a squawk of irritation.

"Cramp," she announced. "Such a bore, darlings. I need more practice. But guess what I saw while I was up there? Sails! We have visitors."

"SAILS?" Pom and Billy were open mouthed, and Jangle emerged from his bucket.

"That's what I said, my petals." Angelina pranced round in a circle.

"Were they coming from Strüggen?" Pom asked. "From the south?"

Angelina waved a claw. "North AND south."

"But why have they come?" Pom stared out to sea. Squinting into the sunlight, she was almost certain she could see distant sails. "They've never come before."

Jangle jumped to his feet. "It's Queen Planchette, come to rescue me!" Forgetting all his terrors, he arranged his gold chain carefully. "About time too. I'm very important, you know. I'm Prime Minister of Thrum!"

"And I expect your father's coming to find you,"

Billy told Pom.

Pom bit her lip. "Billy… What if they start fighting each other? Father hates Thrum! He's always going on about how greedy they are, and how he'll declare war the minute he sees their warships out on the Dillyman Sea."

Billy took a moment to think. Then, stepping forwards, he whispered in Angelina's ear. She looked startled and shook her head.

"But you said you'd do anything to repay us," Billy reminded her. "And just think: you've spent over a hundred years keeping Strüggen and Thrum from fighting each other. Now's your chance to finally make them see sense." He saw Angelina was listening with interest, and went on, "If they see you with Pom and Jangle, they won't be scared of you, or try to attack you."

The dragon gave him a thoughtful look. "You might have a point, dear boy. Very well … I agree. We'll fly high together in order to demonstrate peace, love, unity and friendship."

Pom's eyes shone. "Oh! How WONDERFUL!"

"Fly?" Jangle began to shake. "No. Oh no, no… I won't. I won't, I won't, I WON'T, I tell you!"

Pom fixed him with her steeliest gaze. "So you're too much of a coward to try to save your country?"

Jangle gawped at her. "What?"

"I mean," Pom said haughtily, "that you have an obligation to your queen. If you don't join us, she's more than likely to declare war on Strüggen … if Strüggen hasn't declared war first, of course."

"But I can't!" Jangle began to wail. "I'm terrified of heights. I'll die!"

Angelina sniffed loudly. "Despicable behaviour."

Billy, more sympathetically, pulled his handkerchief out of his pocket and handed it to Jangle. "Here – blow your nose. We'll think of some other way."

Jangle snatched at the hankie and sank his face in it. "Thank you," he said. "I wish I was brave, like you … and … and…" His eyelids fluttered, his head drooped – and Billy was only just in time to catch him before he collapsed.

As Pom grabbed his other arm she whispered, "That was the hankie you used for the blue mushroom, wasn't it?"

Billy went pale. "Oh no! I forgot."

Pom grinned at him. "But it's just what we needed, Billy Boiler! Let's get him onto Angelina's back. You'll have to come too and hold him on."

She shook Jangle hard and he opened one bleary eye.

"Listen to me, Mr Prime Minister. You're going to have a wonderful dream. You're going to dream that you're flying and that you're incredibly brave. Now keep walking..."

Jangle's eyes closed again, but a faint smile crossed his face as Pom and Billy marched him towards Angelina. "Brave," he murmured. "I'm very brave—"

SPLASH!

The explosive sound of a cannon being fired into the water shook them all. Angelina jumped, Billy and Pom went pale, and even Jangle quivered.

Pom quickened her pace. "Hurry!" she hissed at Billy.

A minute later they were airborne. Billy was gritting his teeth as he hung on to Jangle, but Pom was in ecstasies. Angelina, weighed down by her passengers, muttered, "Peace, love and unity! Be strong, Angelina … you can do it!" as she flapped her way slowly upwards.

Looking down, Pom could see her father's warships steadily advancing from the South and as they flew higher she could see the fleet from Thrum approaching the far side of the little island.

Leaning forward, she whispered in Angelina's ear – and Angelina chuckled. "Whatever you say, sweet thing. Let's welcome the Queen of Thrum!" And she swooped into a long curving dive.

The Thrum sailors ran in all directions, shouting and ducking for cover, but on the flagship one lonely figure stood firm. Queen Planchette was gazing up at the dragon and her riders; as they passed above her head Billy lifted Jangle's arm in what he hoped looked like a merry wave.

The queen stared, burst into peals of laughter and waved back.

"What's that white flag mean?" Billy had to shout to make himself heard against the rush of the wind.

"It means they come in peace!" Pom yelled back. "And now for Father."

As they swept away, Jangle began to murmur and to rub his eyes.

"You're dreaming," Billy told him. "Keep your eyes closed. You don't want to wake up yet… It's the best dream ever."

Jangle sighed and was quiet.

The warships from Strüggen had nearly reached the island by the time Angelina got back to the southern shore. The king was standing in the prow of his favourite ship, and to Pom's surprise she saw her mother and brother beside him.

Behind them was a group of soldiers, armed to the teeth; as Angelina flew nearer they raised their guns and Pom gasped. "They're going to fire!"

"And ruin my beautiful scales, darling? Not if I can help it." Angelina plummeted down, smoke streaming from her flaring nostrils.

The soldiers took one look and leapt into the sea. The king clutched the queen … and Dribble caught sight of Pom. His mouth opened wide in astonishment before he began to scream at the top of his voice.

"It's not FAIR! I want to ride a dragon! Bring it here NOW!"

But Angelina was already heading back to Bullion Island.

As Angelina landed, Jangle fell off. He immediately curled up and went on sleeping; the dragon ignored him, and looked at Pom and Billy.

"Sweet things," she said, "I've been thinking. I might be wrong, but I suspect the people of Strüggen and Thrum might be just a teensy weensy bit upset when they find out there isn't any gold."

Pom sighed. "Father will be furious."

"As I thought." Angelina nodded. "So how would it be if I took it upon myself to tell a tiny little fib?"

"What kind of fib?" Pom asked.

"Well..." Angelina hesitated. "You came to the island looking for a dragon, didn't you? And you found one. A poor lonely dragon, living a sad and pathetic life."

Pom nodded. "And the stories about gold just weren't true?"

Angelina beamed at her. "Exactly!"

"Oh." Pom turned to Billy. "What do you think? Should we pretend there wasn't any treasure?"

"Yes," Billy said firmly. "Because if we tell them what we did, there's sure to be someone who'll try to get the gold out again—"

"—and there'll be lots more arguments about who it really belongs to." Pom finished his sentence for him – and Billy looked sad.

"Maybe one day kingdoms will learn to share things."

"Maybe," Pom said. "And when they do, we'll tell them everything." She took Billy's hand. "We'll tell them together, Billy Boiler. We're going to be married one day, remember. We'll tell them when I'm queen and you're king."

Chapter Fifteen

Angelina was exceedingly gracious when introduced to Queen Planchette, King Vigor and Queen Hyacinth. Arranging herself to her best advantage on a rock, she announced that she wished to make a little speech.

"My dear visitors! You should be proud of your young people." King Vigor and Queen Hyacinth looked doubtful, and Angelina repeated, "VERY proud! Their bravery brought us together and history has been made."

Pom and Billy blushed; Jangle, now awake, puffed out his chest and rattled his gold chain of office.

Angelina settled herself more comfortably. "Allow me to tell you my story. A terrible storm blew me to Bullion Island when I was a mere draglet, and I've been here ever since. Thrum and Strüggen are far away, and even though I might have managed the journey I knew all too well how I would be received. We dragons have an unfortunate reputation, and you would have met me with fire and fury long before I was able to reveal my secret … the secret that I, Angelina, am a truly exceptional dragon. Although gifted with the power to breathe fire and smoke, my principles forbid me to harm a living being."

Angelina sighed dramatically, and a single silver tear trickled down her cheek.

"Mine has been a long and lonely life, my darlings. The only ship ever to visit here belonged to a pirate – I believe his name was Jed Josiah Jones—" Queen Planchette, King Vigor and Queen Hyacinth leant forward in eager anticipation—"but when I offered my hand in friendship he fled, his crew with him."

"Ahem." King Vigor coughed loudly. "Pirate Jed Josiah Jones, eh? And … erm … what about his treasure? Excuse me for asking. Left it here, did he?"

Angelina shook her heavy head. "Treasure? You'll not find as much as a single gold coin anywhere on this island." She turned to Pom and Billy. "Am I right, my darlings?"

Pom and Billy nodded, and Jangle, not wanting to be left out, stepped forward with a pompous sniff. "As Prime Minister of Thrum," he announced, "I agree. I saw the cave myself and there wasn't any gold. None at all. It was completely empty."

There was a long silence, finally broken by Queen Planchette. "So we've been wrong all these years. But do you know what? Perhaps it's all for the best." She turned to King Vigor and Queen Hyacinth. "What do you think, dear sir and madam?"

There was another pause before Queen Hyacinth spoke, with a meaningful glare at King Vigor. "I agree. There's been far too much time and money – *especially* money – spent on wars and ships. I suggest we shake hands and make friends."

King Vigor opened his mouth, looked at his wife and closed it again. He nodded and held out his hand to Queen Planchette, who shook it with enthusiasm.

Angelina began to purr, and Pom and Billy smiled at each other. Jangle looked smug, but Dribble pulled at his mother's arm.

"I want a ride on the dragon," he demanded, "and I want it NOW!"

The queen held up a warning finger. "Dribble, be quiet. I have something to say to Persephone. Persephone, we missed you. Yes. Of course, a note saying where you'd gone would have been helpful. Luckily for us a fisherman reported you'd not come back with his boat. Gone with a lad … is this him?"

Pom pulled Billy forward. "Billy Boiler, meet my mother."

Queen Hyacinth, with no sign of recognition, gave Billy a regal nod. "How-de-do. It seems you and my daughter have solved a nasty problem. Please consider yourself welcome at Strüggen palace, any time."

King Vigor coughed. "Ahem. Yes. Most welcome. And Persephone … *ahem*. Yes. Well done." He gave Pom an awkward pat on the back before Dribble pulled at his sleeve.

"WANT A RIDE ON THE DRAGON!" The prince, purple in the face, was now jumping up and down, and the king turned to Angelina.

"Madam Dragon… Would it be possible, do you think, to do us a favour?"

"Indeed!" The queen nodded. "Could you give our precious darling boy a little ride?"

Angelina fluttered her eyelashes. "Thank you, dear majesties, thank you. A dragon's reputation for fiery destruction is a cruel burden to bear, but at last you know me for what I am: a humble bringer of love, peace and harmony. I would be only too delighted to give you all a tour round my island." She gave her visitors, some of whom

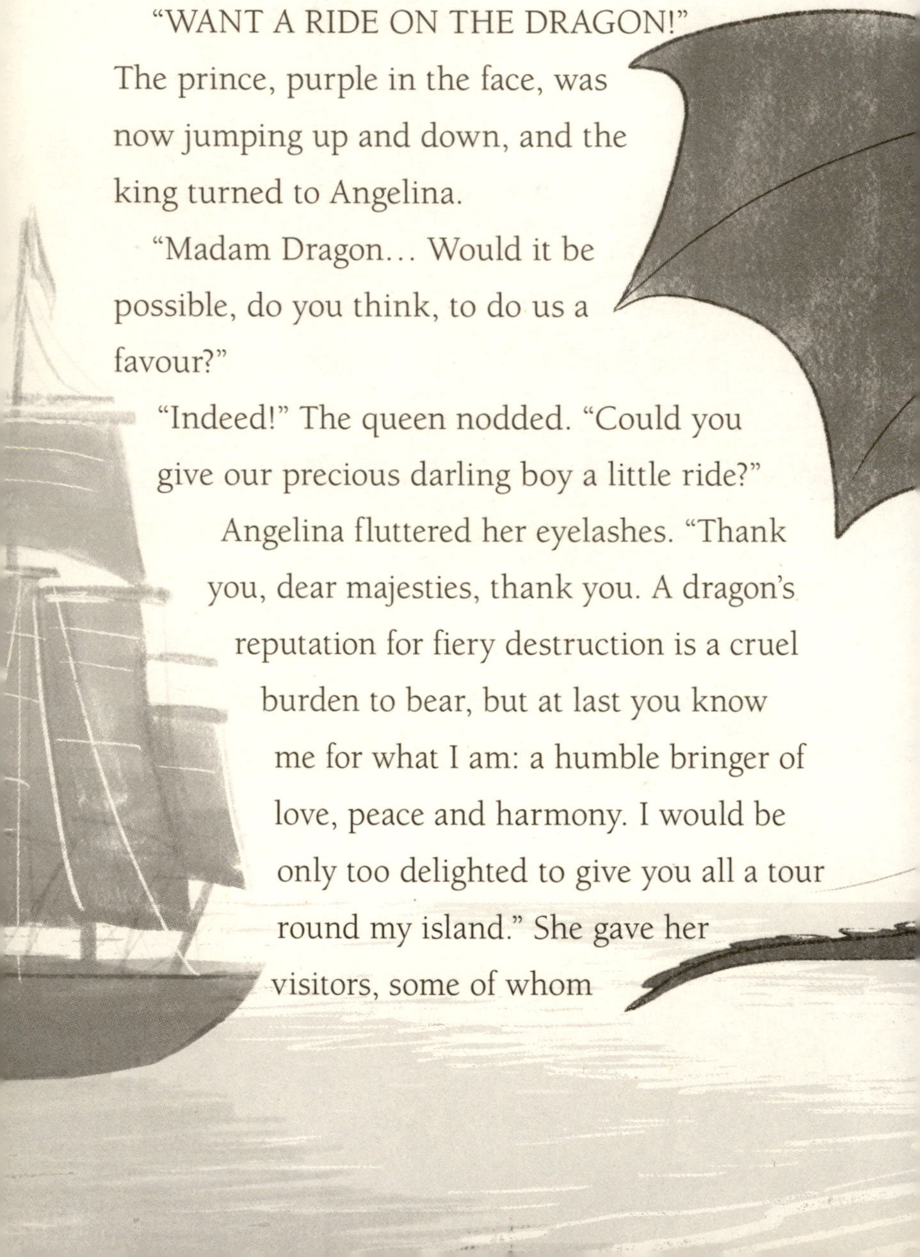

were substantial in size,
a thoughtful glance.
"Two at a time,
perhaps?"

As the royal visitors
eagerly accepted, Pom
drew Billy to one side.
"Come on," she said, "let's go."

"Don't you want to stay with your parents?" Billy asked in surprise.

"No." Pom tucked her arm through his. "It seems they do care about me after all … a bit. But look at them now! They've forgotten me already and Angelina's loving the attention. Let's get the boat."

Billy was happy to agree and they walked down the beach together. The boat was where they had left it and the Mumble was sitting waiting for them. "**Boatie-boat,**" it said cheerfully. "**We is come for ride in boatie-boat!**"

"Of course you can – but you'll have to get off the oars first," Pom told it.

The Mumble shook its head. "**Friend will help! Been talking. Look! Turtle!**"

Pom and Billy looked, and as Alberta waved a flipper Pom flung out her arms in greeting. "My darling turtle! Oh, Billy! Isn't that just too wonderful? Alberta's the best turtle in the whole wide world … and she can take us anywhere we want. Let's go exploring!"

Billy grinned, but a thought came to him. Picking up a stick, he wrote a message in the sand. "Gone exploring. Home for tea. Princess P and Billy B."

"Hurry up, Billy!" Pom called, and Billy dropped his stick and ran to join her.

After all sorts of mayhem, **TALLULAH TICKLE** has one last chance to keep her place as a witches' apprentice. She must prepare a mouth-watering midnight feast in just three days – and wicked witch Gertrude is plotting against her! With help from her brother Tom, can Tallulah whip up something special before time runs out?

ALFIE ONION is setting out on a great adventure. His brother Magnifico is off to make the family's fortune … and Alfie's carrying his luggage! But it turns out Magnifico hates adventures and Alfie has to save the day – with a little help from his loyal dog, a talking horse, two mice and some meddling magpies.

PRINCESS PEONY has a bad feeling that her father might be a tyrant. She doesn't want to believe it, but he has a nasty habit of throwing people in dungeons…There's a royal party coming up, and the king's in an even worse mood than usual. He flat out refuses to invite the wicked hag, which can mean only one thing: TROUBLE!

Vivian French

lives in Edinburgh, and writes in a messy workroom stuffed full of fairy tales and folk tales – the stories she loves best. She's brilliant at retelling classic tales, as she did for *The Most Wonderful Thing in the World*, and has created worlds of her own in *The Adventures of Alfie Onion*, *The Cherry Pie Princess* and *Tom & Tallulah and the Witches' Feast*. Vivian teaches at Edinburgh College of Art and can be seen at festivals all over the country. She is one of the most borrowed children's authors in UK libraries, and in 2016 was awarded the MBE for services to literature, literacy, illustration and the arts.

Marta Kissi

is a wonderfully talented illustrator, who came to Britain from Warsaw to study Illustration and Animation at Kingston University, then Art and Design at the Royal College of Art. *The Dragon's Breakfast* is her fourth book with Vivian French; her other work for children includes books by Sophie Kinsella, Gillian Cross and Olympian Mo Farah. She shares a studio in London with her husband and their pet plant Trevor.